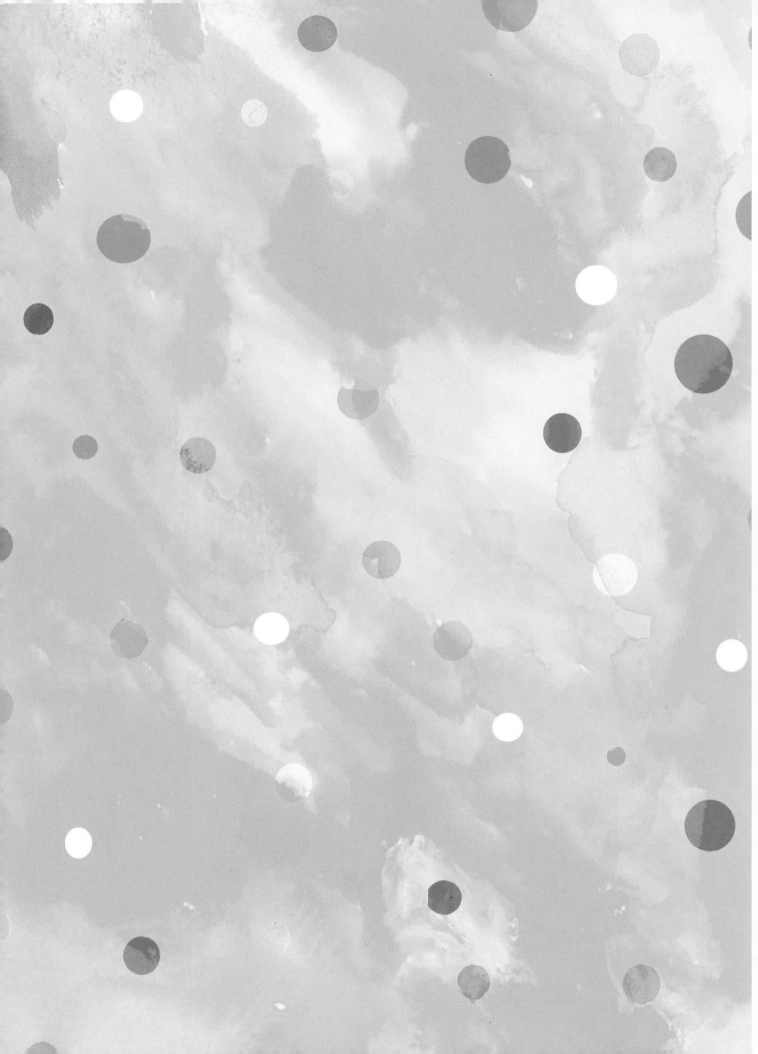

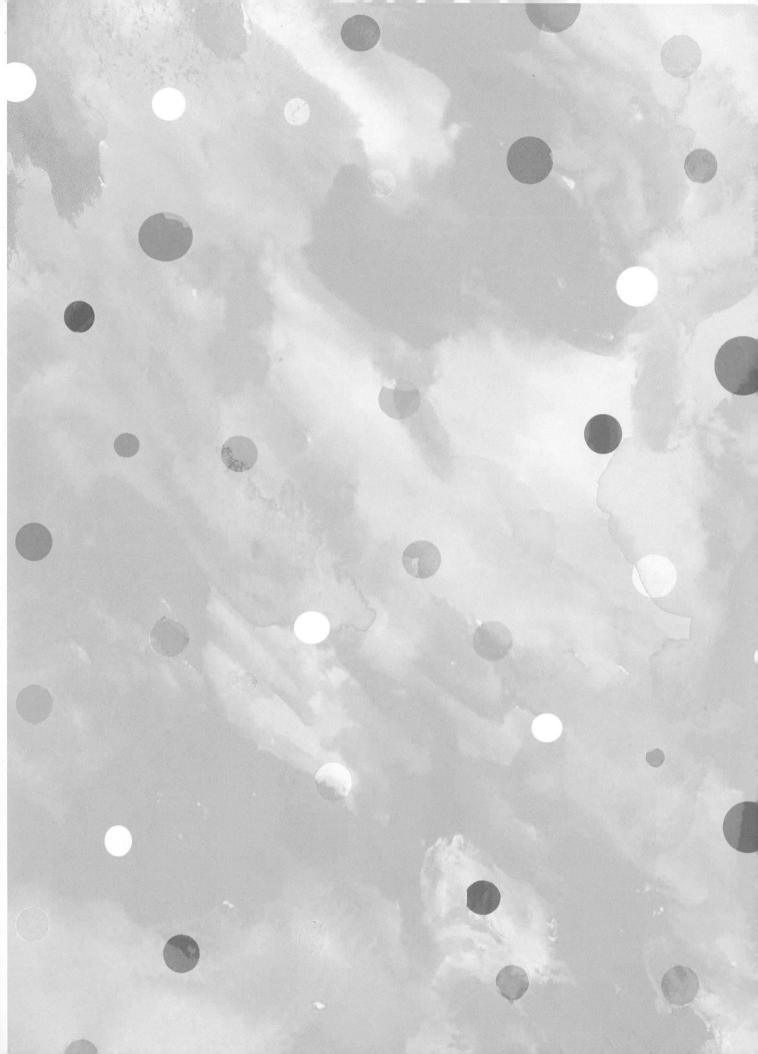

Mella's Box

Story and Illustrations by Hannah Marie Povroznik

DORRANCE
PUBLISHING CO
EST. 1920
PITTSBURGH, PENNSYLVANIA 15238

Dorrance Publishing Co
585 Alpha Drive
Pittsburgh, PA 15238
Visit our website at www.dorrancebookstore.com

ISBN: 978-1-6470-2019-4
eISBN: 978-1-6470-2035-4

To my father,
who is the anchor to my life,
a sail to guide my dreams,
and a beacon to light my path.

A Plain Brown Box

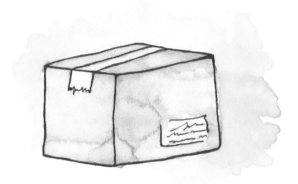

Chronic hunger is not a single story. Rather, it plagues families, schools, and communities. Sometimes poverty fights a silent battle with people nearest to the heart. My family has had the privilege of sponsoring six children through Compassion International, an organization devoted to providing humanitarian aid to children living in poverty around the world. It is humbling. Over the years, I witnessed the impact of proper nutrition. Smiles appeared in photographs, and artwork exploded with imagination.

Stories from children a world away inspired me to cultivate change in my small town nestled among the mountains of West Virginia. Known for its friendly people, rich history, and natural beauty, it is a beautiful place to call home. Throughout its scenic landscapes and among its communities, food insecurity exists. People struggle with hunger everywhere in the United States. According to the United States Department of Agriculture, 41 million people are food-insecure meaning they lack consistent access to nutritious food due to insufficient resources. Nearly 13 million of these individuals are children. In 2017, I founded Boxing It Up to Give Thanks to raise awareness of hunger on a local level. Its mission was to provide families with a complete boxed Thanksgiving meal with a turkey and all the traditional holiday accompaniments. The vision behind Boxing It Up to Give Thanks was to eliminate food insecurity for one day, leaving more time for families to do what families do best – make memories!

With a dream, a voice, and three years of determination, Boxing It Up to Give Thanks raised $60,000 to package 2,044 boxed Thanksgiving meals, providing 41,000 pounds of food to nearly 12,200 individuals across 34 food pantries in seven counties. May the story of Mella's Box serve as a reminder of the power of a single idea and the impact a community can make. Everyone is fighting something. We can make a difference. Change can start anywhere at any time. Let that be here and now!

The sun peeked through the curtains.
With a moan and a groan, Mella flopped
out of bed.

Her belly grumbled. At the thought of
food, Mella thumped down the stairs.

In the kitchen, Mella peered at
the table and inside cabinets too.
Sadly, they were bare.

"I am sorry, honey," Mom said with a frown, "but we will have a warm meal together at the mission this evening."

In math, the teacher said with a smile,
"Let's learn about numbers."

$$1 \times 1 = 1$$
$$2 \times 4 = 8$$
$$3 \times 3 = 9$$
$$6 \times 2 = 12$$

$$\frac{1}{4} +$$

Mella's belly roared.
The rumbling within
made it too hard to think.

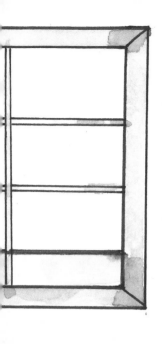

At lunchtime, she had an idea...
  "Oliver, would you care to share a cracker?" questioned Mella.
  "No," responded Oliver. "I am hungry as can be."

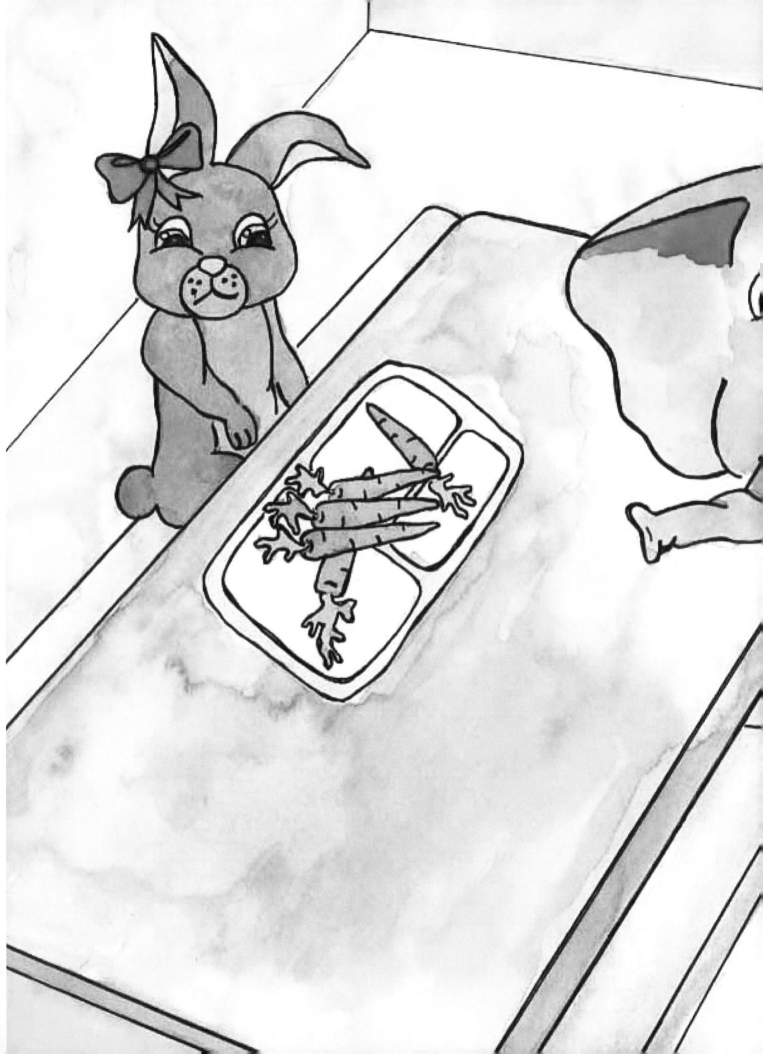

Before giving up, Mella went to the next table...

"Willow, could you spare a carrot or two?" Mella asked with a sheepish smile.

"Sorry. These are all for me," replied Willow.

At the end of the day, Mella trudged home. The closer she got, the more her excitement grew.

Her mom was waiting at the door and called, "Are you ready for dinner?" Mella jumped with joy and shouted, "Yes! Yes! Yes!"

They walked to a little building where warm meals were provided. Mella strolled through the line. Then, she saw two familiar faces.

Oliver and Willow were serving food.

Mella quickly turned and ran! Feeling embarrassed, a tear rolled down her cheek.

"Wait!" shouted Willow. "We are sorry. We didn't know."

"Please come back. We can sit and eat together," added Oliver.

Mella thought for a moment. Oliver and Willow were concerned and wanted to help. "Thank you," she gladly accepted.

Oliver asked, "Will we see you next week? We are handing out boxes of food for Thanksgiving."
Mella's smile grew larger, and she replied, "That's so kind!"

Mella counted the days.
Then, it was finally time. With
a whoop and a holler, Mella ran
into the kitchen.

There stood Mama with a big box. "Your friends Oliver and Willow just dropped this off!"

Opening the box, Mella grinned with delight. She found a turkey, stuffing, sweet potatoes, pie, and so much more!

Mella could not hide the feeling inside her. She was grateful and blessed. This day was the best!

A Message from the Author

Mella was created in honor of my NaNa, Carmella Marie Povroznik. She lost her battle with liver cancer when I was nine. As a child, I remember her gentleness, wisdom, and steadfast belief that life has a way of working itself out.

Boxing It Up to Give Thanks was a project that I prayed would inspire and provide a force of hope and unity in my community. Mother Teresa said, "I alone cannot change the world, but I can cast a stone across the waters to create many ripples." What began as a small project is gaining momentum across several counties in my state. May Boxing It Up to Give Thanks encourage others to give back because, friends, we have a world to change!

Acknowledgments

Many thanks to those who have supported, encouraged, and mentored me along the way. Thank you to my Dad for being my inspiration. You truly have a heart of gold and eyes that see infinite possibilities. I am so grateful for your love, guidance, and the way you bring laughter to any situation. To my Mom, you are my favorite proofreader and will forever be my Grammar Guru.

A special thanks to Price Cutter for assisting with food purchases and serving as our storage, packaging, and distribution center. Your kindness and compassion spearheaded a journey that has impacted many.

A sincere thank you to my corporate sponsors. Without your financial support, this project would not have been possible. Thank you for believing in a 15-year-old girl with a dream in her head and passion in her heart!

100+ Women Who Care Harrison County, About You Monograms, Abraham Linc Corp, Advantage Solutions, American Legion Auxiliary Unit, American Legion Post 68, Antero Resources, Artworks, Asphalt Kings LLC, Bear Contracting, BJ Services, Black and White Ice Cream Shop, Bridgeport Express Care, Bridgeport High School Key Club, Bridgeport High School Student Council, Bridgeport Lions Club, Bridgeport United Methodist Church Members, Buffalo Wild Wings, Card My Yard, Christine's Hot Spot Lounge, Clear Mountain Bank, Diamond Street Car Wash, East Coast Underground LLC, Ed Dean – MVB Mortgage, First Baptist Church, Freedom Kia, Harry Green Nissan, Jenkins Ford, Jenkins Subaru, Kindermusik, McDonald's, Muriale's Restaurant, Pantry Plus More, Radiology Physician Associates, St. Mary's Grade School, Star Furniture, State Farm, Steptoe & Johnson PLLC, Tenmile Land LLC, TGI Friday's – Bridgeport, WV, The Caboose, Thrasher Engineering, United Hospital Center Federal Credit Union, Wells Fargo, and WVU Medicine-United Hospital Center Staff.

To the rest of my village who contributed in both large and small ways, I thank you! The world is a better place because of people like you who share your time, talents, and financial support to mentor young leaders like myself. Thank you!

To the Key Club International Youth Opportunities Fund, thank you for awarding Boxing It Up to Give Thanks a grant to promote awareness of food insecurity to children.

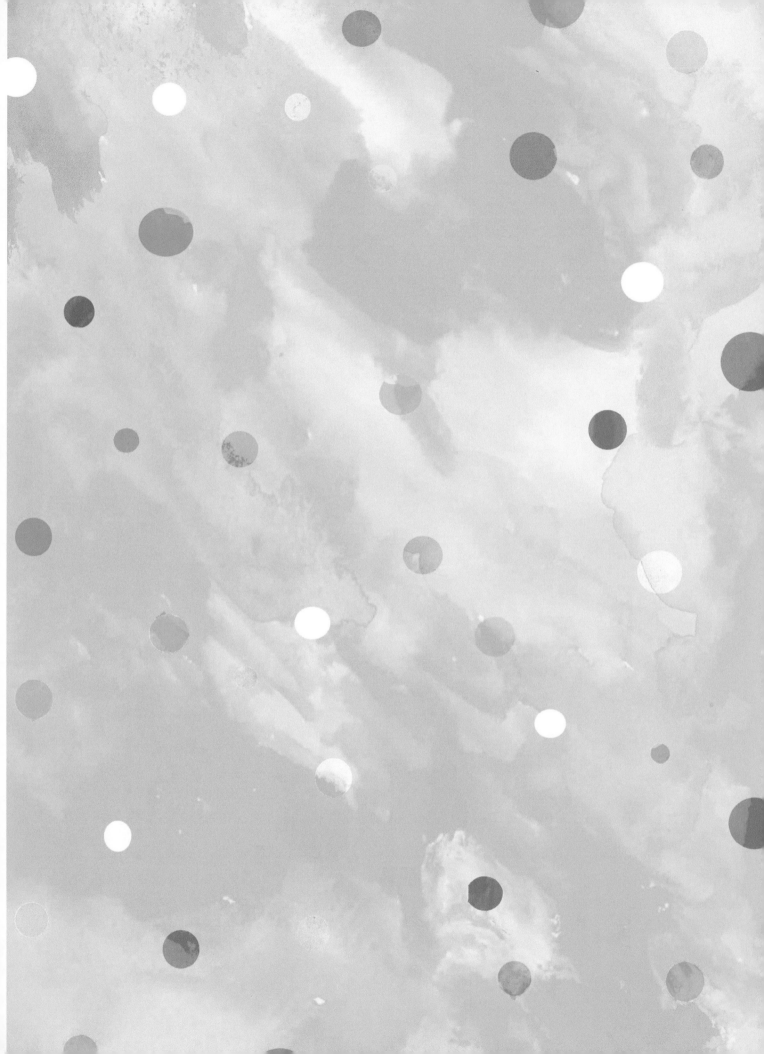

CPSIA information can be obtained
at www.ICGtesting.com
Printed in the USA
BVHW050153011020
589923BV00002BA/7